Dear Parents:

Congratulations! Your child is taking the first steps on an exciting journey. The destination? Independent reading!

STEP INTO READING® will help your child get there. The program offers five steps to reading success. Each step includes fun stories and colorful art or photographs. In addition to original fiction and books with favorite characters, there are Step into Reading Non-Fiction Readers, Phonics Readers and Boxed Sets, Sticker Readers, and Comic Readers—a complete literacy program with something to interest every child.

Learning to Read, Step by Step!

Ready to Read   Preschool–Kindergarten
• big type and easy words • rhyme and rhythm • picture clues
For children who know the alphabet and are eager to begin reading.

Reading with Help   Preschool–Grade 1
• basic vocabulary • short sentences • simple stories
For children who recognize familiar words and sound out new words with help.

Reading on Your Own   Grades 1–3
• engaging characters • easy-to-follow plots • popular topics
For children who are ready to read on their own.

Reading Paragraphs   Grades 2–3
• challenging vocabulary • short paragraphs • exciting stories
For newly independent readers who read simple sentences with confidence.

Ready for Chapters   Grades 2–4
• chapters • longer paragraphs • full-color art
For children who want to take the plunge into chapter books but still like colorful pictures.

STEP INTO READING® is designed to give every child a successful reading experience. The grade levels are only guides; children will progress through the steps at their own speed, developing confidence in their reading. The F&P Text Level on the back cover serves as another tool to help you choose the right book for your child.

Remember, a lifetime love of reading starts with a single step!

For M.E.C., E.A.P., Ricky, Andrea,
and the rest of the politicos at KMS/KHS
—C.H.

For Kurt, Margot, and Gwyneth,
who always have my vote
—E.T.

To Dave, who won my vote
with his charisma and tech support
—D.P.

Visit us on the Web!
StepIntoReading.com
randomhousekids.com

Educators and librarians, for a variety of teaching tools, visit us at RHTeachersLibrarians.com

Library of Congress Cataloging-in-Publication Data
Names: Hapka, Cathy, author. | Titlebaum, Ellen, author. | Palen, Debbie, illustrator.
Title: How not to run for class president / by Cathy Hapka and Ellen Titlebaum ; illustrated by Debbie Palen.
Description: New York : Random House, [2016] | Series: Step into reading. Step 4
Summary: "Third-grader Will's little brother Steve enthusiastically manages Will's campaign for class president, despite Will's total lack of interest in running"— Provided by publisher.
Identifiers: LCCN 2015030048 | ISBN 978-1-101-93362-6 (trade) |
ISBN 978-1-101-93364-0 (hardcover library binding) | ISBN 978-1-101-93363-3 (ebook)
Subjects: | CYAC: Elections—Fiction. | Schools—Fiction. | Brothers—Fiction.
Classification: LCC PZ7.H1996 Hor 2016 | DDC [E]—dc23
LC record available at http://lccn.loc.gov/2015030048

Printed in the United States of America
10 9 8 7 6 5 4 3 2

This book has been officially leveled by using the F&P Text Level Gradient™ Leveling System.

Random House Children's Books supports the First Amendment and celebrates the right to read.

How Not to Run for Class President

by Cathy Hapka and Ellen Titlebaum
illustrated by Debbie Palen

Random House 🏠 New York

Little Brothers and Other Bad Ideas

Hi, my name is Will.

One Sunday, I was eating popcorn and reading comic books.

Suddenly my younger brother, Steve, poked me.

"I want you to walk Buster with me," he said. "It's more fun when we do it together."

"Good idea," Dad said. "Go with him, Will."

"But—" I began.

"Just go," Mom said. "You could use some fresh air, Will."

Steve ran outside.

I shuffled out the door, holding Buster's leash.

"Look at this, Will!" Steve cried. "Your class is electing a president!"

"So? All the grades do that," I told him.

"Not kindergarten," Steve said. "I wish we were having an election, too. Are you going to run for president? It would be fun to be in charge!"

"It's not about being in charge," I said. "It's about doing a lot of extra work."

On Monday morning, Chelsea rushed into homeroom.

"Mr. Duffy, may I present my new campaign idea?" she asked.

"Go ahead, Chelsea," Mr. Duffy said.

Chelsea smiled at the whole class. "Everyone loves a good book, right?"

We all cheered.

"Cool! This is my plan," Chelsea said.
"Reading to kindergartners! We'll be like
big sisters and brothers. And you'll only
have to give up a little bit of free-reading
time each week to do it!"

Everyone was still cheering—except me.

Kindergartners?!? Steve was in kindergarten!

"Great idea, Chelsea!" my friend Jack called out.

"Yes, it is an excellent idea," Mr. Duffy said. "Does anyone else want to present any campaign ideas? Remember, the election is this Friday."

"Nobody else is running, Mr. Duffy," a boy named Luke said.

"Wait a minute," I said. "Is everyone really okay hanging out with kindergartners?"

"What do you mean, Will?" Jack asked.

"I live with a kindergartner," I said. "Trust me, they're not that much fun."

Everyone stared at me.

"Don't be mean, Will," Chelsea said. "Your little brother is great."

"Yeah, great at being annoying," I said.

Lesson #1: When it comes to campaign promises, you're never going to please everyone.

Me and My Big Mouth

At soccer practice that afternoon, Steve
and his friends were playing right next to
our game.

Chelsea passed me the ball, and I was
just about to score.

But suddenly—

"Look out!" Jack yelled. "Stray ball!"

It was Steve's, of course.

"Sorry, Will," Steve called.

"That's okay, Steve," Chelsea said with a laugh.

"No, it's not," I muttered. "Go back to your own game, Steve."

"Don't be a meanie, Will," Chelsea said.

"That's easy for you to say," I told her. "You don't have a little brother. You don't know what they're really like."

"Lighten up, Will," Jack said.

But I wasn't finished.

"And now you want me to spend even *more* time with Steve," I reminded Chelsea.

"Everyone else liked my idea," she said.

"Everyone else is crazy!" I exclaimed.

"Give it a chance, Will," Chelsea said.

"I'm not going to give it a chance," I yelled. "I'm not going to let you do it— even if I have to run for class president myself!"

Does your mouth ever move faster than your brain? Mine just had.

"Hey, Dad!" Steve yelled. "Did you hear that? Will's running for president!"

Uh-oh.

My dad hurried over, beaming.

"That's great, Son," he said. "I was class president once myself."

My heart sank. How was I going to get out of this?

"I'll be your campaign manager, Will," Steve said. "This will be epic!"

Lesson #2: When it comes to big decisions, think before you speak.

The Campaign Begins

That night, not even my favorite comic book made me feel better.

"Hey, Will," Steve said. "Let's talk strategy. First we need to get your name out there."

"Go away, Steve," I said.

"Okay, I'll brainstorm and get back to you." Steve skipped off to his room.

The next morning, I was hungry for pancakes.

"Where's Grandma?" I asked. "I was hoping she'd make me breakfast."

"She's driving Steve to school," Mom said. "He wanted to get there early today."

Uh-oh. This couldn't be good. . . .

I was right. It wasn't good. In fact, it
was worse than I could have imagined.

21

How could I ever show my face in school again?

"Hey, Will!" Jack yelled. "Your posters are awesome!"

"Yeah," said a fifth grader I barely knew. "Way to go, Will!"

Luke pointed at a poster.

"Even Chelsea couldn't get rid of baked beans," he cried. "You're the best, Will!"

I couldn't believe it. Maybe running for president wasn't so bad after all.

Lesson #3: Any publicity is good publicity.

23

Promises, Promises

Chelsea came over, frowning.

"Get serious, Will," she said. "You're promising stuff you can't deliver."

I wasn't sure what to say. Luckily, Steve dragged me away.

"Hey, Will," he said. "Come meet some very important supporters from my class.

They promise they'll vote for you as many times as they can if you play soccer with them once a week."

"Only third graders can vote in the third-grade election," I told Steve. "Besides, nobody is allowed to vote more than once."

The kindergartners looked disappointed.

"Does this mean you're not going to play soccer with us?" Steve's friend Abigail asked.

"Don't worry," Steve whispered. "We'll work something out."

That afternoon, Buster came to school with Mom.

"Check out Will's dog!" Jack exclaimed.

"I wish Buster could come to school every day," Abigail said.

"Great idea," Steve said. "Actually, that's Will's latest campaign promise. From now on, every Friday is Bring Your Pets to School Day! It starts this Friday."

"Hooray!" everyone cheered.

"Can I bring my pet tarantula?" Abigail asked.

Chelsea smiled. "I wonder what Principal Smiley will say about this," she said.

I gulped. "Hold on, everyone," I said.

But nobody was listening.

"How's the campaign going, boys?" Dad asked the next morning.

"Great!" Steve said. "I have a super new idea."

"What idea?" I asked.

Steve just smiled. "That's on a need-to-know basis," he said. "You worry too much, Will. You'll find out later."

Steve was right. I worried all day.

After school, I saw a crowd of kids gathered around Steve.

"Vote for Will!" Steve yelled.

"Yeah!" Abigail shrieked. "He's the sweetest candidate!"

Then they started throwing something.

"Candy!" kids yelled. "Awesome!"

"Not awesome," Mr. Duffy said sternly. "You aren't allowed to bribe people into voting for you, Will."

The next day after school, I wanted to play soccer.

But Steve had other plans.

"Hey, everyone!" Steve yelled. "My brother, the future president, is going to make a speech!"

"I—I am?" I stammered.

Everyone was staring at me. I had to say something.

"Tell them all the substitute teachers will be former Olympic champions from now on," Steve whispered.

"Can I still bring my cat in on Friday?" a girl asked.

"No," I said. "But if you like animals, um, maybe we could raise money for the animal shelter in town."

"Great idea," someone said.

"Yeah," Steve said. "But listen to this—if Will is president, no more tests ever!"

The crowd went wild.

Chelsea walked over.

"The test thing won't work, you know," she said. "But I like your animal shelter plan. You have some good ideas when you aren't trying to be popular, Will."

I felt bad. I could tell that Chelsea really wanted to be president and help people.

"Will! Will! Will!" the crowd chanted.

There was just one problem. Thanks to Steve, I was going to crush Chelsea in the election tomorrow.

Lesson #4: Don't promise more than you can deliver.

33

The Big Day

Friday was the big day.

    "Here are your talking points for today's assembly," Steve said while Mom was driving us to school. "You've done the hard part; now let's win this thing."

34

Mom peered out the windshield. "Is that a goat?" she said.

Uh-oh. Apparently some kids had believed Steve's Pet Day promise.

"What's going on here?" Principal Smiley exclaimed. She grabbed a kid with a parrot. "Who told you to bring your animals to school?"

The kid pointed at me. "Will did!"

I gulped. Chelsea stepped forward.

"This was just a misunderstanding,"
she said. "We'll help you find a safe place
for the pets to stay. Right, Will?"

The assembly started out okay.
My speech went pretty well, even though
I didn't use all of Steve's talking points.

Then it was Chelsea's turn. As soon
as she started to speak, Abigail

screeched, "Will is great! Vote for Will!"

Soon everyone joined in.

"Settle down, people!" said Principal Smiley. "It's not a fair election unless all the candidates get to speak."

Chelsea's speech was really good. Everyone else seemed impressed, too.

Then I noticed Steve and Abigail sneaking toward the door. What were they up to?

Soon we all found out.

"Stampede!" Abigail shrieked as the pets raced into the auditorium.

By the time the teachers rounded up all the animals, I was totally fed up with Steve. This wasn't how an election was supposed to be!

"Okay, everyone," Principal Smiley said. "Each candidate will make a closing statement. Then we'll vote."

My closing statement was last.

"Don't forget to promise pizza and a movie every Thursday," Steve whispered.

I ignored him. I knew what I wanted to say. "I hereby take back all my crazy

campaign promises," I said loudly. "If you vote for me, the only thing I'll promise is to do what's right for the whole third grade."

Steve looked horrified. But Chelsea seemed impressed.

"Do you mean that?" she asked.

Before I could answer, Principal Smiley stood up.

"Time to vote," she said, sounding tired.

Lesson #5: Doing the right thing is never the wrong idea.

The Results Are In

While the other students voted, Chelsea and I had time to talk.

"I'm sorry things got so out of hand," I told her. "And I meant what I said just now. I won't go through with any of Steve's crazy ideas."

Chelsea smiled. "I'm glad you came to your senses," she said.

"The third-grade results are in,"
Mr. Duffy said. "It's a landslide."

"Will! Will! Will!" Steve chanted.

Mr. Duffy shook his head. "The winner
is—Chelsea!"

"What?" Abigail shrieked.

"Congratulations, Chelsea," I said.

And I really meant it. I was a little
embarrassed, but mostly relieved.

"Thanks, Will," Chelsea said. "You were
a worthy opponent. I'd love to make you
my vice president. Together we could make
this the best third grade ever!"

"Sure," I said. "That sounds cool."

I couldn't believe everything had turned out so great.

Then Chelsea turned to Steve.

"Hey, Steve," she said. "I loved your energy on the campaign trail. How would you like to help me with the Reading Buddy program? You'd get to work closely with me and my new VP."

"I'll do it!" Steve yelled. "Isn't this awesome, Will? Now we get to be together all day at school, too!"

Lesson #6: Win or lose, you can't get rid of your little brother!